A Sing-Along Story

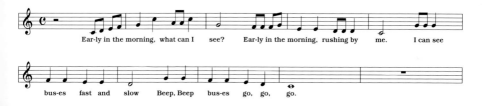

Ear-ly in the morning, what can I see? Ear-ly in the morning, rushing by me. I can see bus-es fast and slow Beep, Beep bus-es go, go, go.

A Publication of the World Language Division

Story written by: Judith M. Bittinger

Director of Product Development: Judith M. Bittinger

Executive Editor: Elinor Chamas

Editorial Development: Elly Schottman,
Kathleen M. Smith, Susan Hooper

Production/Manufacturing: James W. Gibbons

Cover and Text Design/Art Direction: Taurins Design
Associates, New York

Illustrator: Steven Mach

ISBN 0-201-85310-8
11 12 13 14-PX-03

Addison-Wesley Publishing Company

Early in the morning,
What can I see?
Early in the morning,
Rushing by me.

I can see buses
Fast and slow.
Beep, beep, buses.
Go, go, go.

Early in the morning,
What can I see?
Early in the morning,
Rushing by me.

I can see dump trucks
Fast and slow.
Rumble, rumble, dump trucks.
Go, go, go.

Early in the morning,
What can I see?
Early in the morning,
Rushing by me.

I can see skateboards
Fast and slow.
Roll, roll, skateboards.
Go, go, go.

7

Early in the morning,
What can I see?
Early in the morning,
Rushing by me.

I can see shoppers
Fast and slow.
Hurry, hurry, shoppers.
Go, go, go.

9

Early in the morning,
What can I see?
Early in the morning,
Rushing by me.

I can see big trains
Fast and slow.
Clack, clack, big trains.
Go, go, go.

Early in the morning,
What can I see?
Early in the morning,
Rushing by me.

I can see tugboats
Fast and slow.
Toot, toot, tugboats.
Go, go, go.

13

14

Bye, bye city.

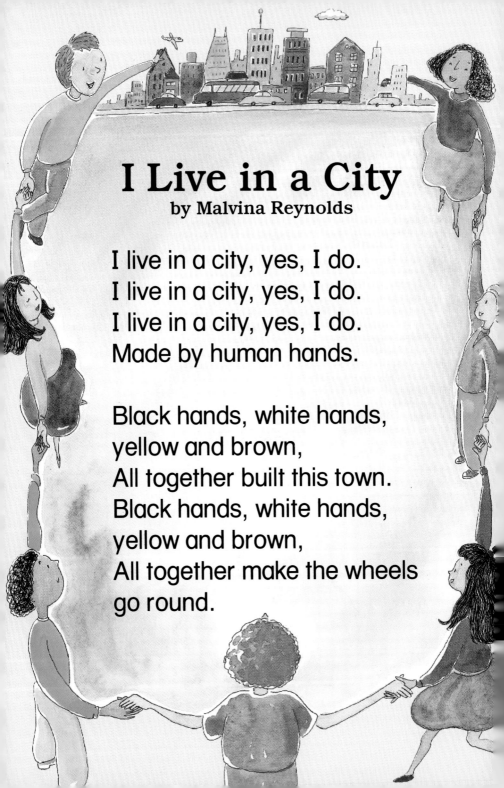

I Live in a City
by Malvina Reynolds

I live in a city, yes, I do.
I live in a city, yes, I do.
I live in a city, yes, I do.
Made by human hands.

Black hands, white hands,
yellow and brown,
All together built this town.
Black hands, white hands,
yellow and brown,
All together make the wheels
go round.